METAL BABY

METAL BABY

STEPHEN W. MARTIN

Illustrated by

BRANDON JAMES SCOTT

Margaret K. McElderry Books

New York   London   Toronto   Sydney   New Delhi

MARGARET K. McELDERRY BOOKS

An imprint of Simon & Schuster Children's Publishing Division

1230 Avenue of the Americas, New York, New York 10020

Text © 2024 by Stephen W. Martin

Illustration © 2024 by Brandon James Scott

Book design by Greg Stadnyk © 2024 by Simon & Schuster, Inc.

MARGARET K. McELDERRY BOOKS is a trademark of Simon & Schuster, Inc.

Simon & Schuster: Celebrating 100 Years of Publishing in 2024

For information about special discounts for bulk purchases, please contact Simon & Schuster Special Sales at 1-866-506-1949 or business@simonandschuster.com.

The Simon & Schuster Speakers Bureau can bring authors to your live event. For more information or to book an event,

contact the Simon & Schuster Speakers Bureau at 1-866-248-3049 or visit our website at www.simonspeakers.com.

The text for this book was set in F25 Executive.

The illustrations for this book were rendered digitally.

Manufactured in China

0224 SCP

First Edition

2 4 6 8 10 9 7 5 3 1

CIP data for this book is available from the Library of Congress.

ISBN 9781665924931

ISBN 9781665924948 (ebook)

For Lola and the number 11.
-Stephen W. Martin

For Perley James and Betts.
Stay frosty.
-Brandon James Scott

The Mumfords were a quiet family

who lived on a quiet street in a very quiet neighborhood.
They enjoyed quiet things like crochet, crossword puzzles,
and classical music.

So you can imagine their surprise when they brought home a
METAL BABY!

The Mumfords tried their best to quiet his cries.
They bought him pacifiers, mountains of plushies,
and even a pair of velvet pj's, but everything just
made him more METAL!

They took him on car rides, train rides, even hayrides!

They burped, bounced, soothed, and swaddled. . . .

But nothing worked!

The Metal Baby was getting louder
and louder and **LOUDER!**
And attracting a LOT of fans.

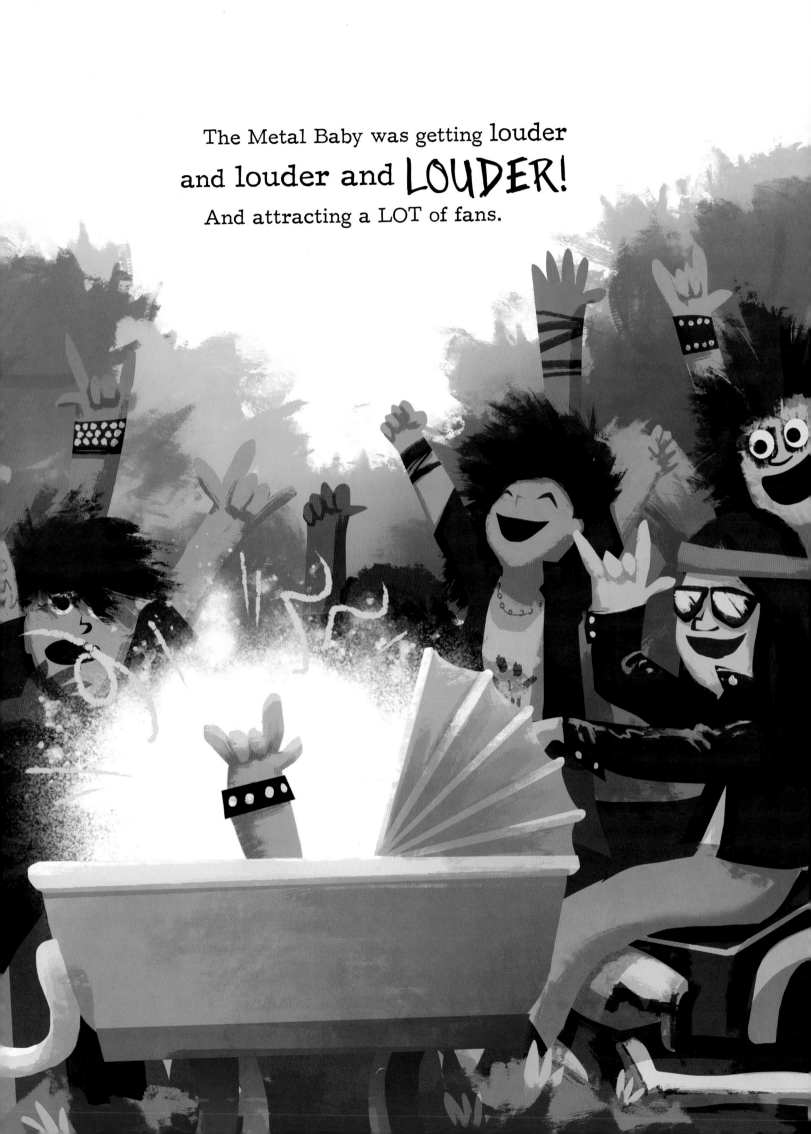

In a last-ditch effort, the Mumfords
even brought in an expert to help. . . .

But they really should have checked her references.

Just when the Mumfords thought it couldn't get any worse . . .
Metalpowerpalooza announced its headliner!

METAL POWER PALOOZA

3 DAYS OF
NONSTOP METAL MAYHEM
FEATURING

METAL BABY WITH SPECIAL GUEST **METAL CAT**

LIVE FROM THE MUMFORDS' BACKYARD!

Their Metal Baby played all day and all night, stopping only to drink!

ANOTHER!

The Mumfords were exhausted.
It took all their strength just to remain standing.

Their quiet souls were crushed like their flower garden.

And that's when it hit them!

The one thing they never tried.

The one thing their Metal Baby loved.

As they smashed their violas onto the stage, the impossible happened. . . .

And the crowd went . . .

QUIET!

It was music to their ears.

ENCORE!

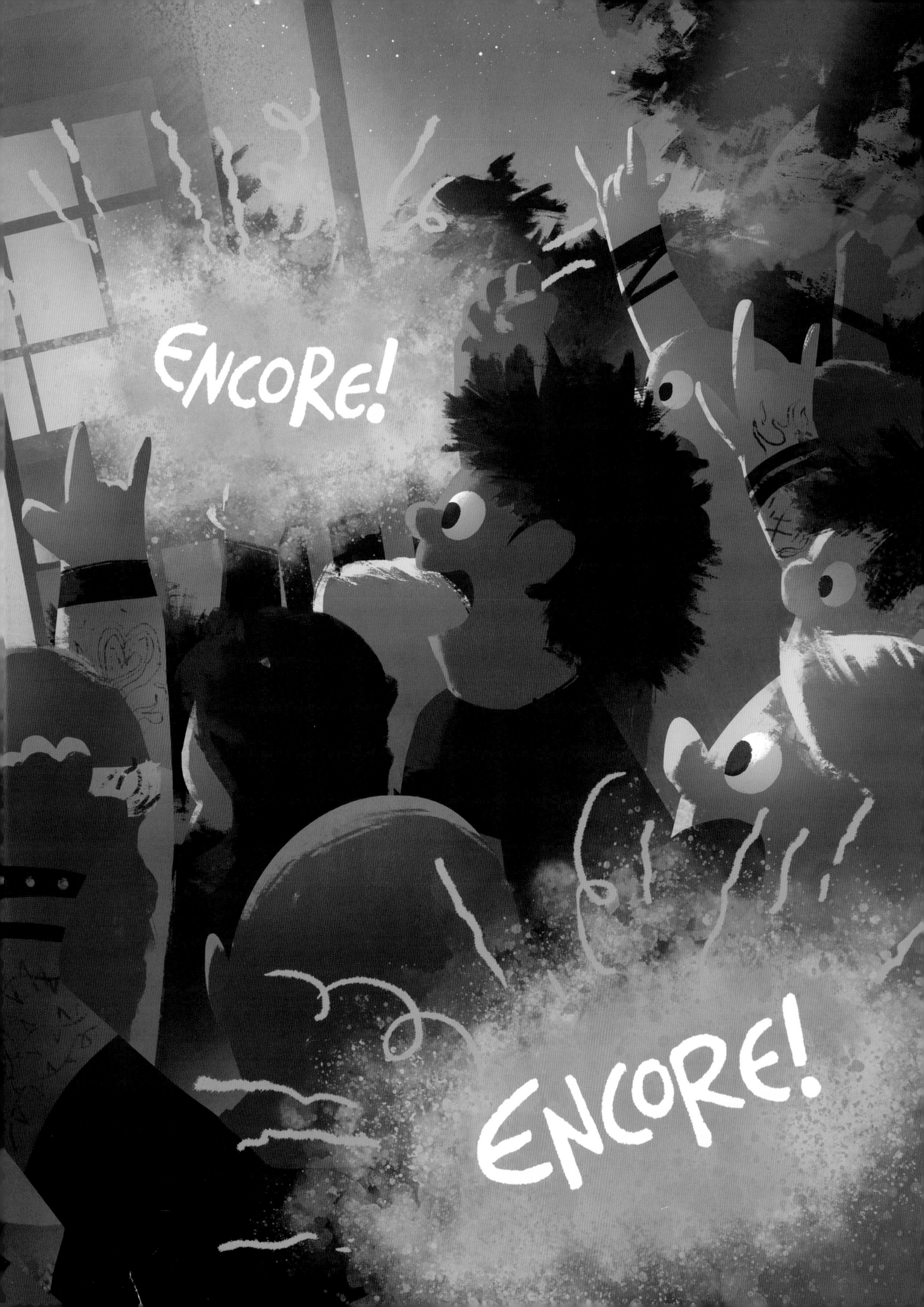
ENCORE!
ENCORE!